Family History

Ebeneezer, the lanky, cool, black cat often wondered why he had such a passion for the sea. After his last adventure as a stowaway on board a sailing yacht racing across the Atlantic Ocean, he returned home to his parents in Belfast.

Ebeneezer had lots of questions to ask his parents. He curled up beside his father on a sunny doorstep overlooking Belfast Lough and listened intently to what his father was telling him about his great, great, great, grandfather Felix.

Felix was born in East Belfast and spent most of his time at Harland and Wolff's shipyard. At that time they were building the world's largest passenger ship called the Titanic.

The shipyard workers were very kind to Felix and brought him food every day. They took great pride in their work and told Felix that the man who was in charge of the design team for the big ship was called Thomas Andrews.

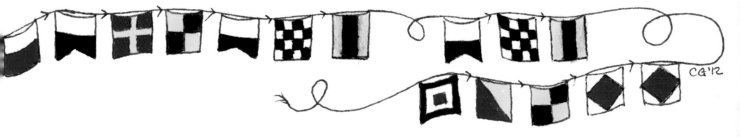

The ship was designed with fifteen transverse watertight partitions and claimed to be unsinkable. Titanic was 825 feet long, with 3 huge propellers, 4 very tall funnels and a speed through the water of approximately 24 miles per hour.

Once the hull of the ship was launched, Felix spent many happy hours watching all the internal fittings being added to the huge empty ship. After the majestic main staircase was in place, he was able to explore the splendid promenades, the palatial apartments, the gymnasium, Turkish Baths, swimming pool and the great dining saloon.

One day in early March 1912 when the ship was almost ready to leave Belfast, the chief engineer spotted Felix lying beside one of the boilers in the engine room. He bent down, stroked Felix and said, "Puss cat, you have been around so much during the completion of this ship, I would like to take you with us on our maiden voyage to New York. Look, I have bought you a special leather collar with a gold tag with your name on it". The engineer carefully fastened the collar around Felix's neck.

Felix told his wife Maisie about the exciting news and at the beginning of April Maisie and their young kittens were amongst the crowds of spectators lining both sides of the River Lagan to watch the Titanic leave Belfast.

Titanic was taken in tow by powerful tug boats and everyone cheered as she was towed out into the channel, bound for Southampton, where many more passengers boarded the great liner.

Titanic made two more ports of call at Cherbourg in France and Queenstown near Cork in Ireland, before setting sail across the Atlantic Ocean bound for New York.

"Oh, Father tell me more about what the inside of the great ship was like," pleaded Ebeneezer.

Chapter 2

Inside the Titanic

Ebeneezer's father rolled over and stretched out his front paws on the doorstep. "I am so pleased that you are so interested," he replied. "I will tell you as much as I can."

Ebeneezer snuggled up close on the doorstep and listened intently to his father.

"Titanic was divided into areas for 1st Class passengers, which were sheer luxury with crystal chandeliers and rich wood panelling. You would have loved the extravagant comfort Ebeneezer!"

Ebeneezer purred at the thought.

"There were also state rooms for 1st Class passengers and cabins for 2nd and third class."

"Can you explain to me what made the power to drive the big ship through the water?" asked Ebeneezer.

"It was driven by huge steam engines which had lots of boilers with furnaces powered by coal," replied his father.

Chapter 3

Disaster at sea

"Father, you told me that the Titanic was supposed to be unsinkable, so what caused her to sink?" inquired Ebeneezer.

"On the night of 14th April 1912 the Titanic collided with the submerged spur of an iceberg that ripped a gash 300 feet along her starboard side about 10 feet above the keel. This let sea water into six of her forward compartments. It all happened so quickly. Within ten minutes the water had risen fourteen feet above the keel in five of the compartments. By midnight the lower deck was submerged," his father replied sadly.

"How terrible! What happened next?" cried Ebeneezer.

"Captain Smith and his officers and crew informed all the 2,201 passengers that Titanic was going to sink. They should make their way as quickly as possible to the lifeboat decks, wearing warm clothing and they had to take their lifejackets too," his father explained.

"Did Captain Smith call the lifeboat and other ships nearby to come and save them?" asked Ebeneezer.

CG'12

"Of course, but remember they were out in the Atlantic Ocean too far away for lifeboats. In those days there were no mobile phones. Long distance messages between ships were sent by Morse code. At that time a man called Marconi had recently developed Marconigrams. They were wireless messages that could be sent between ships and from ship to shore. Many of the 1st Class passengers wanted to try out these new Marconigrams by sending messages to their friends ashore, to let them know what a wonderful time they were having on the Titanic.

When Captain Smith requested that distress messages needed to be sent out, the wireless operators were very busy. They did not realise that the distress messages were urgent," explained his father.

"How strange!" exclaimed Ebeneezer.

"Well everyone had claimed that Titanic was unsinkable. That was why the distress signals were not transmitted for over half an hour after the collision with the iceberg occurred."

S O S

... --- ... (In Morse code)

Chapter 4

SOS

"Did any ships pick up the distress messages?," asked Ebeneezer.

"Several ships did get the distress messages but they were a very long way away and it was out of range for any lifeboats. The Cunard liner CARPATHIA which was bound for Liverpool, from New York, did receive the message and immediately turned. She steamed at full speed in the direction of the Titanic but it was 58 miles away," said his father.

"Did the Carpathia get there in time to save the passengers and crew?" asked Ebeneezer.

"Sadly no. Titanic was sinking very fast. There were not enough lifeboats on the ship for all the passengers and crew. Many passengers jumped into the icy water as the ships stern rose out of the water. She slowly sank bow first."

"By 2.20am the Titanic had disappeared below the surface. It wasn't until daylight that the first lifeboat of survivors was picked up. The rest of the lifeboats were scattered over 5 miles and it took a further six hours before the Carpathia had picked up all their survivors. Unfortunately, your Great, Great, Great, Grandfather Felix did not survive in the icy water.

In all 711 survivors were saved. That was only a third of all the people who were on the Titanic," recounted his father.

"What a terrible disaster!" cried Ebeneezer.

Chapter 5

Locating the wreck

"Has anyone ever tried to find the wreck or raise it from the seabed?" questioned Ebeneezer.

"Oh yes. There was an American ocean explorer called Dr Robert Ballard. He was keen to find the world's most glamorous shipwreck, which was alleged to be 12,000 feet below the surface. In 1977 Robert Ballard's dream of finding the Titanic began to come true," answered his father.

"What do you mean?" exclaimed Ebeneezer.

"Well, Dr Ballard, with the help of the American Navy, developed a remote control mini submarine pod called 'Argo'. This could be lowered to the seabed. Pictures of the seabed could then be relayed by fibre optic cable to the surface. Then in 1985 Dr Ballard with the help of the Navy found the position of the Titanic 13,000 feet below the sea with his mini submarine 'Argo'."

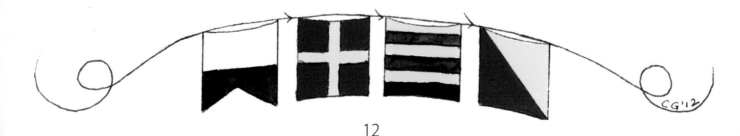

"How amazing!" screeched Ebeneezer. "Are they going to be able to raise the wreck to the surface?"

"Oh no, the relatives of all those lost on Titanic consider it to be a grave and it should be left as it lies on the seabed. There is very little light or life at that depth. It is very quiet and peaceful, a very fitting resting place for the remains of this greatest of sea tragedies," his father told him.

Chapter 6

Ebeneezer makes plans

"Is it possible for anyone to go down to view and inspect the wreck or is it too deep?" asked Ebeneezer.

"Yes. There is a Russian research vessel called 'Keldysh', that has two strange mini submarines, attached to either side of the boat by projecting arms. They looked like space craft. This vessel went to the site of the wreck.

There divers entered the mini submarines which were then lowered on the arms and towed away from the vessel. While the mini submarines descended in a corkscrew motion, the divers were able to talk to the crew on the ship because the salt in the sea can conduct radio waves.

Once they were two and a half miles down, they could see the famous bow of the Titanic looming out of the darkness. They had powerful 5,000 watt lights to enable them to explore the wreck."

"Wow!" cried Ebeneezer, arching his back and extending his tail straight up into the air. "Father, I now know where I want to go for my next sea adventure. I want to go down in one of those mini submarines to see the Titanic".

"That sounds like mission impossible," remarked his father, "although I can tell you that in 2005 a Northern Ireland BBC reporter did go down in one of the mini submarines to view the wreck and to place, Harland and Wolff's plaque on the deck because they were the company who built the ship. Ebeneezer do you know that fewer people have dived to the Titanic, than have been to outer space?"

"In April 2012 it will be 100 years since the Titanic sank. To commemorate the centenary a company called 'Deep Ocean Expeditions' in America are planning to take 80 people down, two at a time, to visit the wreck. This will be the only time that tourists will be able to make the trip. Some people have already signed up and paid a lot of money for their trip. Ebeneezer, it would be very difficult for you to get into one of those mini submarines without anyone seeing you." remarked his father. "It's getting late and I am tired after telling you all I know about the Titanic."

"Thank you, Father. Let's go inside and see if there is some food left out for us. Then I can sleep on my idea and work out a plan tomorrow," said Ebeneezer.

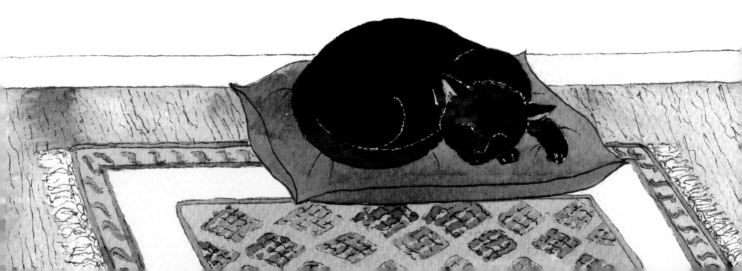

Chapter 7

The plan takes shape

The next morning, Ebeneezer, was up and out on the prowl very early. He went quickly down to the Belfast docks and explored the various wharfs to see if there were any ships bound for New York. Some people were carrying suitcases and walking towards a big cruise liner.

In the distance he could see a huge new silver coloured building which looked like the bow of a ship. There were several construction workmen beginning to start their days work on the building. A huge crane was operating above the roof with a magnificent staircase dangling from it, in the gentle breeze. Slowly it was being lowered down into the building.

Ebeneezer stopped suddenly to listen to the people, who had slowed down in front of him.

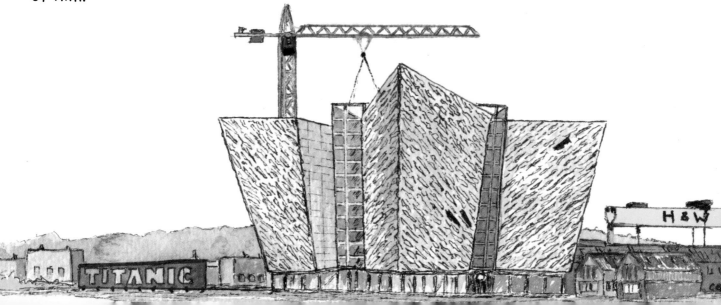

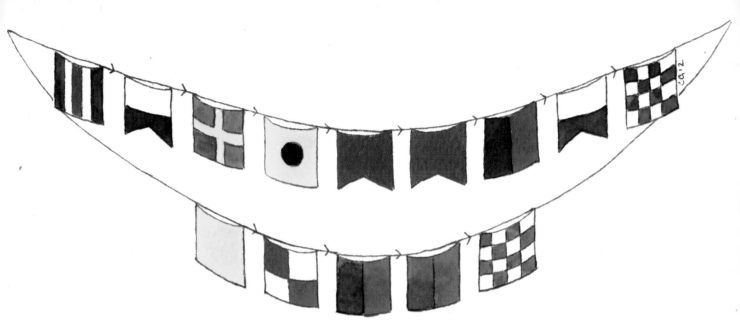

A tall man pointed towards the building and explained to his companion that it was a new visitor's centre where visitors will be able to re-live the Titanic story.

Then he pointed towards an enormous cruise ship further down the dock. "That's the 'Caribbean Queen', the cruise ship that I am going on. She is calling at New York en route for the Caribbean. I have heard she has 800 staterooms, a wedding chapel, four swimming pools, a spa, a gym and a choice of dining rooms. They even have movie shows under the stars in good weather," the tall man explained to his companion.

"Now I know why you wanted me to carry your cases and bags. It was so that I could see the cruise liner you were going away on. What time does the 'Caribbean Queen' set sail?" his companion remarked.

"At midday," the tall man replied.

Chapter 8

Ebeneezer sets off

Ebeneezer didn't wait to hear anymore. He just turned tail and ran as fast as he could back to his father's house. "Father, Father!" he shrieked, "I have found a cruise ship that is setting sail for New York in a couple of hours and I am going to try to get aboard without anyone seeing me."

"Are you sure you really want to go?" questioned his father.

"Yes of course, I just came back to let you know that I will be away for a few weeks," explained Ebeneezer. Then he rubbed his head against his father, purred into his ear and gave him a quick lick. "Wish me, luck !" he whispered before dashing off again in the direction of the docks.

It didn't take him long to reach the 'Caribbean Queen'. Ebeneezer saw two ladies standing at the bottom of the gangway. There were two sports bags on the ground beside them. One was open and only half full. Quick as a flash, Ebeneezer slipped into the open bag and crouched down out of sight.

Two or three minutes later a porter lifted the bags and carried them on board the cruise ship.

"What luck!" thought Ebeneezer as the bag was carried into a very comfortable stateroom.

While the ladies were giving the porter a tip, Ebeneezer crept out of the bag and hid behind a sofa.

A few minutes later a cabin steward came to ask the ladies if they would like breakfast in their stateroom.
"Yes please, that would be lovely and we would like cooked breakfasts at 9am everyday please," replied the older lady.

Ebeneezer was happy because he expected that some remains of the breakfasts would be left on the trays each morning after the ladies had finished and gone on deck. Hopefully this would be enough to feed him, so that he could remain hidden for the five days at sea.

Just then there was a knock on the cabin door and the younger lady opened the door and welcomed her friend James on board. Ebeneezer managed to squeeze under the sofa, so that he was completely hidden.

"Well Lucy isn't this so exciting? The ship sails in about half an hour and in five days we will be in America." Then we can make our travel plans for St. John's in Newfoundland and join the 'Deep Ocean Expedition' to see the wreck of the 'Titanic'." exclaimed James.

"James, don't you think it will be very dangerous to go down in one of those little submarines? I wouldn't want anything to happen to my daughter," questioned Lucy's mother.

"It has been well tried and tested by several people already and you shouldn't have any worries Mrs Brown," replied James.

Ebeneezer stretched out his front paws to make himself more comfortable and listened with delight to the three people chatting about their plans.

Chapter 9

The voyage to New York

When James, Lucy and her mother finished talking about their plans, they left the cabin to go on deck to watch the ship leave Belfast.

"What luck !" thought Ebeneezer as he wriggled out from under the sofa. "I just need to stay close to those people and somehow I should be able to get to St John's." Ebeneezer explored the stateroom carefully and decided the best place to hide was under the sofa. There was a separate bathroom where he could get water to drink but needed to be careful not to get cornered in there if the Browns came back unexpectedly. He climbed up onto a desk below a porthole and looked out. There was a short drop onto a secluded area of deck. Ebeneezer tried the catch on the porthole with his paw and found he could open it without too much difficulty. He looked out but decided it was too risky to go out in case the Browns came back and closed him out.

The ship was now picking up speed as it left Belfast lough behind and Ebeneezer heard footsteps approaching. He quickly returned to his hiding place as Lucy and her mother entered the cabin.

"We are meeting James for dinner in half an hour, so we had better unpack and get changed," said Lucy.

Mrs Brown slowly unpacked and then sat down on the sofa for a rest.

"I will just ask the steward to bring me a light meal here in the cabin because I am tired and am looking forward to an early night. You go on and make your plans with James," she said.

Lucy changed and left to make her way to the dining room.

Soon there was a knock at the door and a steward entered with a tray of food. He put it down on the table and asked Mrs Brown to put it outside the door when she had finished. Mrs Brown ate most of the meal and then went into the bathroom for a shower.

Ebeneezer quickly crept out and pulled a piece of bacon off the tray and pushed it under the sofa. He then went back and lapped up some milk from the jug on the tray.

When Mrs Brown emerged from the bathroom she lifted the tray and put it outside the door.

The next five days passed quite quickly and the seas were calm so Ebeneezer was able to get enough food from the breakfast trays and evening meals, which were brought to the cabin. Most days he managed to jump out of the porthole to have a quick romp on the deck when no one was about and the stewards were cleaning the cabin. The stewards always left the porthole open for a while to air the cabin.

Chapter 10

Next stop Newfoundland

All of a sudden there was a dull thud and lots of American voices started shouting about securing the mooring lines. Ebeneezer knew they had arrived in New York. There were announcements over the tannoy to tell passengers that they could disembark in half an hour once the gangways were in position.

Ebeneezer watched Lucy and her mother pack their bags and once again there seemed to be an half empty sports bag which he managed to sneak inside whilst they were checking to make sure everything had been packed.
James came to the cabin door and picked up the bags and helped Lucy and her mother off the ship.

A taxi was waiting to take them to the ferry for Newfoundland, which is an island belonging to Canada. The ferry trip would take about 36 hours.

Once they were settled in their small cabin Mrs Brown told Lucy that she would be glad to get to St John's and stay with her sister, while James and Lucy went on their expedition to see the wreck of the Titanic. Ebeneezer now knew that he must be careful to make sure he hid in Lucy's bags.

When Mrs Brown and Lucy had left the cabin, Ebeneezer climbed out of the bag and hid in a dark corner of the lower bunk.

They returned after their meal in the café and went to bed. Lucy got into the top bunk and her mother into the lower one. Ebeneezer curled up as small as he could so that Mrs Brown's feet couldn't touch him.

In the morning he watched carefully to see who owned the sports bag he had hidden inside. Luckily it was Lucy's, so when they went for breakfast he crept inside again.

After the ferry docked in St John's they disembarked. There they were greeted by a large jolly looking woman who rushed up to embrace Mrs Brown. Lucy and James also gave her a hug and told her that they would be back from their adventure in about 2 weeks.

"Please take care," Mrs Brown shouted after them as they jumped into a waiting taxi.

A short time later, Lucy and James arrived at the 'Deep Ocean Expeditions' office in St John's.

They were warmly welcomed and shown onto an awaiting coach with several other people. Luckily, Lucy placed the bag on the floor under the seat in front of her, so that Ebeneezer was out of sight and could stretch and arch his back. The coach soon set off for the short journey to the large ocean going boat which was to take them approximately 380 miles South East of Newfoundland to the site of the wreck of Titanic.

When the coach arrived at the dock, the group boarded the vessel and were allocated cabins. James and Lucy had planned to share a cabin, so they put their bags inside and went off to explore the ship. Ebeneezer was happy to be able to get out of the bag and stretch his legs. He was very hungry and managed to get out of the cabin because Lucy had not closed the door properly. He could smell food cooking in the galley further along the passage. Carefully he counted the number of cabin doors between Lucy's cabin and the galley, so that he could find his way back.

Suddenly he heard three blasts on the boats whistle. All the passengers and crew were being summoned for a safety drill. Ebeneezer crouched behind a fire extinguisher, while lots of passengers and crew went to their muster stations.

Soon the passage was deserted and he was able to sneak into the galley and fill his empty stomach with lots of delicious food. Back in the cabin he curled up in the corner behind a curtain and fell asleep.

Chapter 11

Discovered at last

Ebeneezer awoke with a start when James and Lucy returned to the cabin. The vessel was underway and seemed to be making good speed.

"I can't believe we are almost there," said Lucy. "It has always been my ambition to see the wreck ever since I was told that my Great, Great Aunt drowned on the Titanic. I wonder when we will get to the diving area?"

"They say it will take about 6 days. There will be lots of lectures about the dive and preparations for us to do, so that when we arrive we will be ready," answered James.

The next morning James happened to pull back the curtain and a startled Ebeneezer jumped up and rubbed himself against James's leg.
"Hey Lucy look what I found !" he exclaimed, "this must be the ships cat."
"I love cats ! Let's keep him with us for the time being," answered Lucy.

During the rest of the voyage to the dive site, Ebeneezer slept in their cabin. He was able to get out to explore the ship and climb into the hangars to investigate the mini submarines which were stored in them.

James and Lucy brought him food and he listened to all their plans and instructions for the dive.

A few days later excitement was rising as the support vessel anchored to prepare for the dives. Twenty people would be going down 2 at a time. James and Lucy were to be the third couple to go.

"I am glad we are not first. Now we can watch what happens on the first dive." remarked James. "See the small entry hatch into the mini submarine? You have to go down a ladder from the deck to get into it." he said.

"We have been told to eat and drink very little for 12 – 18 hours before we go, and to take plenty of layers of clothing because the temperature changes so much. The dive down is going to take two and a half hours and then we will have 3 – 4 hours to explore the Titanic wreck. The whole trip will take approximately 8 – 10 hours" Lucy reminded him.

The weather was calm and the next morning the first two couples climbed down the ladders into the two mini subs which were lowered by cranes into the sea.

Then they were towed away from the support vessel ready to dive and soon disappeared below the water. The captain said that they would be in constant radio contact with the two mini subs while they were diving and that they would be able to photograph the passengers in each mini sub at the wreck site.

Chapter 12

Mission accomplished

Ebeneezer hid in the hangar overnight and waited until morning when the pilot came to check the mini sub for the next dive. The pilot opened the hatch and went inside to test the instruments. Quick as a flash, Ebeneezer jumped through the hatch and managed to get to the back of one of the bunks and hide under a rug. The inside was very tiny and cramped, with only one window at the front where the pilot sat at the middle of the window. The two bunks were down each side.

Soon he heard familiar voices as Lucy and James climbed down the ladder and through the small hatch into the mini sub. The pilot told them to lie down on the bunks facing the window and to make themselves as comfortable as possible. It would be a long day.

The hatch was closed and secured. The crane lowered the mini sub into the sea and soon it was towed clear of the support vessel. The pilot requested permission to dive and started to pump ballast water into the tanks to start the descent. The mini sub descended about 100 feet per minute.

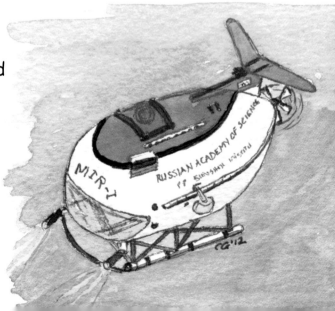

As they descended the water became darker and darker so that soon powerful lights were switched on to illuminate the surrounding water. After another hour or so, a sort of lunar seascape began to emerge.

"Wow !" exclaimed Lucy, "We must be nearly there."

Ebeneezer crept slowly out from under the rug, crawled slowly up the bunk and gently lay across James' shoulders so that he could see out the front of the mini sub. James felt the sudden weight on his shoulders and looked round to see Ebeneezer. He stroked him gently and decided that he was probably used to going down in the mini sub, since he thought he was the ships cat.

Suddenly the bow of the Titanic came into view and, although it was covered in sea weed, the guard rails were clearly visible. The mini sub glided over the top of the wreck and it was possible to see where the grand staircase was once located. It was also possible to see the bridge and promenade areas. The mini sub then moved towards the stern section which had separated when she sank and one of the ship's giant boilers came into view.

There were plenty of old shoes, leather suitcases and other debris strewn across the ocean floor and the pilot told Lucy and James that there would never be any attempts to salvage anything more from the wreckage as the relatives of those who lost their lives wanted it left untouched as a memorial.

Ebeneezer suddenly dug his claws deep into James's shoulder and peered forward because he had seen something shiny tangled up in a piece of seaweed on the ocean floor. James looked down at the seabed and asked the pilot to stop and reverse back a little.

"Look down there Lucy. I can see a gold name tag caught in the seaweed and it says 'Felix, Ships cat, S. S. Titanic'," James exclaimed.

Ebeneezer purred with contentment. He had achieved his ambition to see the wreck of the ship, on which his great, great, great grandfather had lost his life.

Suddenly the pilot looked over at James and exclaimed, "Where did that cat come from? Who gave you permission to bring him on the dive?"

James looked surprised and told the pilot that he thought the cat belonged to the support vessel and was used to doing the dives.

"That's amazing, as I would never have agreed to having a cat on board this mini sub or the support boat" the pilot replied.

"Don't worry, we will take him back to Newfoundland with us, so you don't need to say anything to the Captain when we return to the surface," explained James.

This was music to Ebeneezer's ears and he dug his claws into James's shoulders with contentment. The return journey to the surface seemed quite quick and Ebeneezer was happy to be back in the cabin with Lucy and James, who brought him a big bowl of food.

A few days later they were back in Newfoundland being greeted by Mrs Brown and her sister. Lucy and James told them all about their amazing dive to the wreck and introduced them to Ebeneezer.

"What are you going to do with that poor runaway cat?" asked Mrs Brown.

"I really don't know," replied Lucy.

"I would love to give him a home" interrupted Mrs Brown's sister. "He seems to have great character."

"That would be wonderful because we have grown so fond of him and couldn't think how we could possibly take him back to Belfast," added James.

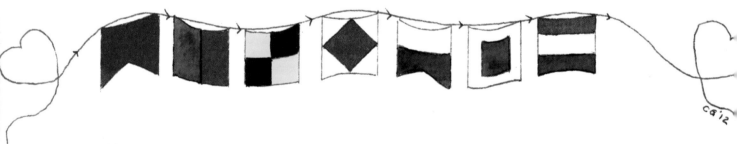

Ebeneezer was so pleased. He knew he would be happy living in Newfoundland with Mrs Brown's sister. That is until he got the urge to go on another sea adventure or had worked out how to get back to Belfast.